AGENT Amelia

GOLDEN CASE FILES

MICHAEL BROAD

Andersen Press
London

First published
in 2011 by
Andersen Press Limited,
20 Vauxhall Bridge Road,
London SW1V 2SA
www.andersenpress.co.uk

The right of Michael Broad to
be identified as the author and
illustrator of this work has been
asserted by him in accordance
with the Copyright, Designs and
Patents Act, 1988.

Printed and bound in Great
Britain by CPI Bookmarque,
Croydon, CR0 4TD

Copyright
© Michael Broad, 2011
All rights reserved.
British Library Cataloguing in
Publication Data available.
ISBN 978 1 84939 327 0

The Case of the
Ghost Diamond   1

The Case of the
Cat-Nappers   45

The Case of the
Whispering Weeds   89

The Case of the
Zombie Cows   133

The Case of the
Perilous Pipe   177

The Case of the
Creepy Cakes   219

I'M AMELIA KIDD and I'm a secret agent.

Well, I'm not actually a secret agent. I don't work for the government or anything, but I've saved the world loads of times from evil geniuses and criminal masterminds. There are lots of them around if you know what to look for.

I'm really good at disguises. I make my own gadgets (which sometimes work), and I'm used to improvising in sticky situations – which you have to do all the time when you're a secret agent.

These are my Secret Agent Case Files.

Ghost Diamond

'What on earth do you have in that rucksack?' Mum said, leaning out of the car window as I heaved the bag off the back seat and onto my shoulders. It was pretty heavy but I tried to pretend it wasn't.

'Stuff,' I said, peering over my sunglasses to gauge her reaction.

'Stuff!' Mum said with a suspicious frown. And the way she said 'stuff' meant she wanted to know exactly what kind of 'stuff', and why I had so much of it.

'Just boring school trip stuff,' I smiled, and legged it for the school gates.

Being vague is the best thing to do when you're under interrogation. Mum would have to really want to know what was in my bag to come after me and continue the line of questioning. I'd deliberately dawdled

back at the house so I knew she was already running late. You have to think ahead when you're a secret agent.

'Well, have a nice time then,'

Mum called out, and then quickly drove away.

Phew!

I couldn't tell Mum my bag was full of secret agent stuff or she'd think I'd gone bonkers. You can't tell anyone that you're a secret agent or else they'd worry all the time when you're off saving the world.

Especially my mum, who gets her knickers in a twist whenever I go to the shops on my own!

My class were
already boarding
the bus to take us
to the museum,
so I stayed at the

back and watched our teacher, Mrs
Granger, ticking everyone off her list.

Mrs Granger had been under
my surveillance for a week and I
was pretty sure she was a criminal
mastermind posing as a teacher. I was
also pretty sure something dodgy was
about to go down at the museum.

Mrs Granger had planned the museum trip so our class could see a famous treasure called the Ghost Diamond, a pendant containing the biggest diamond in the world. Usually school trips are educational, but the Ghost Diamond had nothing to do with our school work so it didn't make sense. Then I snooped around the school library records and discovered Mrs Granger

had recently checked out two very suspicious-sounding books.

One was called *Hypnotism for Beginners* and the other was called *Ancient Jewels and Curses.*

The second one was a very strange subject for a book and bit too much of a coincidence if you ask me!

My teacher was definitely up

to something and I had to get to the
bottom of it.

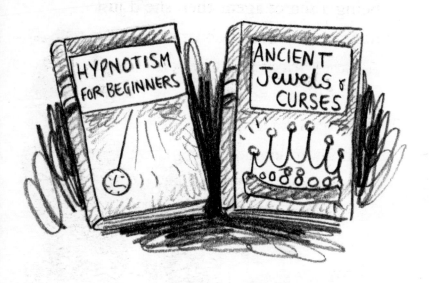

When it was my turn to board
the bus Mrs Granger blocked my way
with her clipboard.

'Amelia Kidd, will you please
take off those ridiculous sunglasses!'
she shrieked, and she shrieked it loud
enough for the whole bus to hear,

so everyone started giggling.

If Mrs Granger suspected me of being a secret agent then she'd just done a very good job of drawing attention away from herself and onto me, which is definitely the sort of thing an evil genius might do.

I took off my sunglasses and Mrs Granger prodded my rucksack with her clipboard.

'And what do you have in that bag?' she said. 'The kitchen sink?'

The whole bus giggled again, but I didn't lose my cool.

'My packed lunch and my big winter coat,' I lied. Well I did have my packed lunch, but not my winter coat. 'Mum said I have to take a coat because it might turn chilly.'

If a teacher starts questioning you, I've found it's a very good idea to blame everything on your mum, then they can't say anything about it and they would never bother to phone up and check.

'Sunglasses *and* a winter coat,' Mrs Granger said, waving me onto the bus with an exhausted sigh. 'Amelia Kidd, you really have come prepared!'

The other kids giggled again as I made my way down the aisle to the back of the bus, but under my breath I said, 'Yes, Mrs Granger, I've come prepared.' And slipped my sunglasses back on. Inside the museum I was keeping a close eye on Mrs Granger when I noticed she'd switched her shoes! She was wearing bright-pink trainers that looked very new and very odd because the rest of her clothes were all dark and old-fashioned.

I'd never seen Mrs Granger wearing trainers before. She always wore sensible black shoes. This was

another clue pointing
to something big
going down at
the museum. I
had to keep alert
and not let my
teacher know I
was onto her,
or she might
postpone her
criminal activity
for another day.

'I like your trainers, Mrs Granger,' said Trudy Hart, who is always sneaking around the teachers. I don't like Trudy Hart. She's very popular in school and is always mean to people who aren't, like me.

'Why, thank you, Trudy,' said Mrs Granger. 'They're new.'

'They look very pretty on you,' Trudy added with a slimy smile.

'Do you think so?' Mrs Granger asked, turning her heel to admire her new trainers. 'Of course field trips involve an awful lot of walking, so I'm wearing them mostly for comfort.'

'Or to make a quick getaway, more like!' I whispered.

Mrs Granger's head snapped up and she narrowed her eyes at me.

Uh Oh!

Mrs Granger told us to explore

the museum on our own and gave
instructions to meet back at the gift
shop in an hour. After my comment
about the shoes I knew she'd be
keeping an eye on me, but I needed
to keep an eye
on her.

I went
straight to the

ladies' loo and propped a bin against
the door so I wouldn't be disturbed.
Then, in front of the mirror, I

rummaged inside my rucksack and produced a large flowery dress and a plum-coloured wig.

Pulling the dress on over my school uniform, I tucked my hair inside the wig and adjusted everything in the mirror. Once satisfied that I didn't look like me anymore, I slipped my sunglasses back on and headed for the door.

BANG! BANG! BANG!

17

Someone was on the other side of the door trying to get in!

'Amelia Kidd!' said a loud angry voice. 'I demand you let me in this instant!'

It was Trudy Hart! And by the sound of giggling I guessed she had a couple of her equally mean cronies with her. She must have seen me come in. With a quick glance at the barred windows I realised I was completely trapped in the loo!

'My needs are greater than yours because I'm popular!' Trudy squealed and booted the door.

I checked

my disguise in the mirror again, and wondered whether it would stand up to close scrutiny. Sometimes being a secret agent is all about thinking on your feet and taking chances, so I pulled my shoulders back, grabbed my bag and flung the door open.

'Well it's about time . . .' Trudy growled, and then stopped when she saw me.

'What a rude little girl!' I shrieked, in my best impression of a grown-up voice. I eyed Trudy up and down and prodded her with an authoritative finger. 'I have a very good mind to find your teacher!'

Trudy's mouth fell open and
her cronies gawped at me with wide
eyes.

Before any of them could get a closer look, I stormed past like an outraged adult. They didn't say anything or come after me, so I think they were definitely fooled. Which was good because I really did have to find the teacher and work out what she was up to.

I wondered if Mrs Granger planned to steal the Ghost Diamond? And if so, why? Criminal masterminds and evil geniuses are only ever interested in world domination, so what could she want with a silly old pendant?

When I found Mrs Granger she was leaving the gift shop with a small brown bag. This was very suspicious because she'd told everyone to meet there in an hour. Also, nobody goes to the gift shop first, everyone goes afterwards to buy souvenirs because

you can't
buy a
souvenir of
somewhere
you haven't
properly
visited yet.

I hid
behind a
pillar until
Mrs Granger
passed me, then I
followed at a safe distance,
ducking and diving and blending
into the crowd. As I suspected she
was heading for the room with the
Ghost Diamond, and she was looking
around her to make sure no one was
following.

Luckily, I'm used to tracking suspects so she didn't spot me.

In the Ghost Diamond room I made two holes in a guidebook and lurked close behind Mrs Granger, watching her carefully as she studied the jewel. After a couple of minutes she struck up a conversation with the security guard, whose job it was to protect the pendant.

'. . . and why is it called the
Ghost Diamond?' asked Mrs Granger
casually.

Something told me she already
knew and was just killing time, or
trying to distract the security guard.

But he was standing right next to the jewel case so she couldn't do anything without him seeing.

The security guard explained that the white centre of the stone was believed to be the ghost of a very powerful spirit, a spirit who vowed to rule the world with whoever released him from his diamond prison.

Ding! Ding! Ding!

(That's the sound of alarm bells ringing in my head.)

My instinct was right, Mrs Granger did want to rule the world, and now she was inches away from a dodgy diamond that would let her do exactly that!

While I was working all this out, I noticed that Mrs Granger had opened the brown bag from the gift shop and was fiddling with something in her hands. But from where I stood I couldn't actually see what she was doing.

Not wanting to risk getting closer I rummaged inside my rucksack and pulled out my mirror-on-a-stick gadget, which sounds like an odd piece of secret agent equipment, but has got me out of a lot of scrapes in the past.

doing!

I positioned the mirror so I could get a close look at Mrs Granger's hands, and I saw that she had an exact copy of the Ghost Diamond pendant! Mrs Granger must have picked it up in the gift shop, and now she was swinging it from side to side in a very peculiar way.

I was so busy watching my teacher I hadn't noticed the security guard, who by this time had stopped talking and was staring at the fake pendant with a very glazed look in his eyes.

'*Hypnotism for Beginners!*' I gasped.

Mrs Granger turned round and gave me an angry glare, then she sprang into action. With the security guard hypnotised not to notice, she

smashed the lid of the jewel case with her elbow, swapped the pendants over and then scarpered in her new pink trainers.

Shoving the mirror back

in my rucksack, I legged it after her. Although the big dress was weighing me down a bit and it was kind of difficult to see through the long plum fringe of my wig.

Mrs Granger was getting away!

Up ahead I noticed Trudy Hart standing by the gift shop with her cronies. She was my only chance to stop Mrs Granger getting away with the Ghost Diamond and taking over the world.

'Stop her!' I yelled at the top of my voice.

But Trudy just sneered and turned her nose up. I'm not sure whether she knew it was me – or just didn't want to help the angry grown-up who had prodded her with an authoritative finger – but it was obvious she didn't intend to stop the sprinting teacher.

As Mrs Granger neared the exit, I had to think fast.

Pulling the rucksack off my shoulders, I swung it over my head to get up some speed and then lobbed it as hard as I could.

The bag sailed through the air . . .

. . . . and hit the floor at the teacher's feet, the straps tangling around her new pink trainers.

Mrs Granger was running one minute and the next she was sprawled out on the floor, but she continued to slide along the shiny marble like a person-shaped bowling ball, heading straight for Trudy Hart and her cronies.

The girls watched in horror, frozen to the spot like tenpins in a bowling alley about to be toppled.

CRASH!

Skidding to a halt,
I snatched my rucksack
from the heap of groaning
people and slipped away
just in time.

All the non-hypnotised security guards suddenly swooped on Mrs Granger and, because they weren't sure exactly what had happened, they pounced on Trudy Hart and her cronies too.

When you're a secret agent you can't ever take credit for saving the world, or else everyone would know who you are and you wouldn't be secret anymore. So by the time I got back from the ladies' loo, in my normal

clothes and with my normal hair,
Mrs Granger was being carted off by
the police.

All the kids in my class were
waiting on the steps of the museum,
so I wandered cautiously over to
Trudy Hart and her cronies, who
were all looking a bit confused.

'What happened?' I said with as much surprise on my face as I could fake.

One of Trudy's cronies burst into tears and Trudy rolled her eyes.

'Some mad woman attacked Mrs Granger,' she said matter-of-factly.

'Oh,' I said. 'Then why are they taking Mrs Granger away?'

Trudy scratched her head.

'I think maybe she stole something from the gift shop?' she said, although it was obviously just a guess. 'I saw the security guards fighting her for a necklace or something; she seemed very angry.'

'Oh,' I said.

'The school has called our parents to come and collect us . . .' Trudy added, and then stopped and frowned at me. She lifted a hand up to my hair and pulled out a long plum hair!

Uh Oh!

I snatched it back and let a swift breeze carry it from my fingers.

Trudy narrowed her eyes at me and was about to say something when I heard the sound of a familiar car horn. I looked out to the road and saw Mum winding the window

down and waving.

'Gotta go!' I said, and legged
it before she could draw any
conclusions.

I shoved my rucksack onto the
back seat of the car and climbed in
after it. Looking up at the museum
steps I could see Trudy Hart was
still frowning, as though she was
trying to work out if any of what she
suspected was even possible.

'I'm sorry your trip was cut short,' Mum said, eyeing me through the rear-view mirror as we drove away. 'You can't have had time to see anything interesting at all?'

'I guess not,' I said, tipping my glasses and peering over the top.

'And you lugged that big bag around for nothing,' Mum added sadly.

I thought about it for a moment and then smiled to myself.

'Oh, I wouldn't say that,' I said, patting my faithful old rucksack.

The Case of the Cat-Nappers

'Amelia!' Mum yelled. 'What on earth do you think you're doing?'

'Bird watching,' I lied, without taking my eyes off the target.

'The point of binoculars is so you can see them from the ground,' Mum sighed. 'You really don't need to be halfway up a tree. Now come down this instant before you snag your jumper!'

'OK,' I said. 'Just one more minute, I'm watching a very interesting bird.'
I wasn't really watching a bird – I was watching the trap I'd set earlier.

Cats had been mysteriously vanishing down my street. It began with one, which wasn't too suspicious because cats wander off all the time. But then another one disappeared, followed by another, and within a week there were no cats left at all!

I was pretty sure a criminal mastermind was planning to take over the world using stolen cats. They're always doing dodgy stuff like that. So I put my stuffed toy, Tiddles, out on the pavement as bait and waited for the cat-napper to nab it.

Mum continued to moan in the background. Then a white van suddenly turned the corner into our street.

I watched as it slowed to a
crawl outside our house and, quick
as a flash, the back doors flew open,

an arm snatched Tiddles, and the van
screeched away!

Adjusting the focus on my
binoculars, I scanned the speeding
vehicle and saw the words: 'Smith's
Fish' in blue lettering along the side.

The van belonged to the fish

shop around the corner! 'Aha!' I said, because at last I finally had a lead. 'Aha?' Mum inquired as I clambered down the branches.

'Oh, I was watching an Aha Bird building a nest,' I said. 'They're very rare.'

Mum frowned at my jumper and brushed pieces of bark and twigs away with her hand.

'I can't imagine why Gran agreed to knit you a black one,' Mum sighed. 'It really is the worst colour for showing up bits. And besides, black isn't very cheery for a girl of your age.'

'I like it,' I shrugged.

Of course my real reason for choosing black was so that it would come

in handy during night-time
manoeuvres. Also, when you're on
surveillance up a tree in the daytime,

a bright-pink jumper would be a
dead giveaway. You have to think
ahead when you're a secret agent.

Mum was walking back to the house when I suddenly had an idea.

'Can we have fish for dinner tonight?' I asked, tagging along behind.

'But you don't like fish,' she said. 'The last time we had fish you were ill.'

'That was when I was little,' I said. 'I'm pretty sure I like it now.'

'Hmmm, well if you're sure,' Mum

said uncertainly. 'But you'll have to pop to the fish shop for me. I'm not going out again just because you've decided you like fish all of a sudden.'

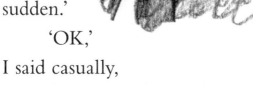

'OK,' I said casually, and slipped on my sunglasses.

On the way to Smith's Fish I discreetly collected 'LOST CAT'

posters from all the trees and
lampposts. Now I knew who'd
swiped the missing moggies I'd need
a list of telephone numbers to return
them.

Outside the fish shop I tucked
the posters into my rucksack and
rummaged around for an appropriate
disguise. Although Mum's mention of

Gran had already given me an idea.

I pulled on an old plastic mac, crammed a short curly wig on my head and tied a see-through plastic rain hood on top of it. It wasn't raining – but old ladies

often wear rain hoods when it's not raining.

A bell rang over my head, wig and rain hood as I tottered into Smith's Fish.

A short plump man hurried out from the back of the shop and glared at me. I guessed this was Mr Smith. He stood over the counter, folded his arms and sighed (as though he had

better things to do than serve old
ladies – things like pinching people's
pets!).

'What do you want?' he
demanded.

'I'd like some fish, please,' I
croaked, hunched over and gazing at
the counter.

There wasn't a lot of fish to

choose from, just a couple of prawns and a crab. I guessed all the stock had been used up keeping the stolen cats happy – and not very successfully judging by the scratches on Mr Smith's hands.

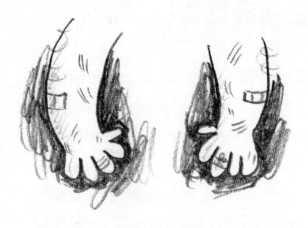

'What kind of fish do you want?' he asked impatiently.

'Two nice pieces of haddock, please,' I said, peering over my sunglasses.

'We're all out of haddock,' he snapped. 'It's either prawns, crab or nothing.'

'Oh, well in that case I'll just have two nice pieces of haddock, please,' I croaked, and while Mr Smith was busy getting irritated I surveyed the shop for any signs of cats. The great thing about the old-lady disguise is you can keep people distracted

for ages while you carry out basic
surveillance.

'ARE YOU DEAF?' he yelled.
'I SAID WE'RE ALL OUT OF
HADDOCK!'

'Yes, haddock,'
I said. 'Two nice
pieces, please.'

This
went on for
a while and
Mr Smith
was getting
very red in
the face, when a short
plump woman suddenly appeared
behind him. I figured this must be
Mrs Smith, and she didn't look very
happy either.

'What's going on out here?' she growled, glaring sideways at her husband.

'This deaf old bag wants HADDOCK!' he growled back.

Mrs Smith offered me an unconvincing smile.

'Then fetch some from out the back!' she snarled.

'But—' said Mr Smith.

'The job's going down tonight, so we won't need it anymore,' hissed Mrs Smith through gritted teeth.

'And you're drawing

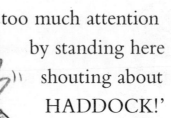

too much attention
by standing here
shouting about
HADDOCK!'
The other
great thing
about the old-
lady disguise is
that people always
think you're deaf –
they whisper things
thinking you can't hear them and
always give vital details away.

Mrs Smith gave me another
fake smile, grabbed her husband by
the elbow and marched him out to
the back of the shop, where they
started arguing. I couldn't hear
exactly what was said, but things like,

'Keep a low profile!'
and, 'Get rid of her!'
filtered into the shop.
The reason
I couldn't hear
them
properly
was
because
I'd leaped
over
the counter and was busy
rummaging through a pile
of papers beside the till –
I was looking for clues to
the exact location of the
cats.

Among the bills
and receipts I found a

strange map-like diagram!

I didn't have time to look properly, but I did see the word 'cat' among the various scribbles. Deciding the map must lead to the cats I shoved it in my plastic mac and crept back around the counter.

Mr Smith suddenly reappeared with a parcel wrapped in white paper.

'Two nice pieces of haddock, madam,' he said politely.

I didn't get a chance to study the map before dinner, so that evening I pretended to have an upset tummy and asked to go to bed early.

'I knew I shouldn't have let you have fish,' Mum sighed.

I shrugged my shoulders helplessly and shuffled off to my room.

Closing my bedroom door carefully I ran to the desk, flicked on the lamp and unfolded the piece of paper. On closer inspection I discovered it wasn't a map at all, it was a blueprint.

A blueprint of the local bank!

There was a diagram etched
over the blueprint with drawings

of cats and arrows pointing in and
out of the bank. I couldn't work
out exactly how, but it was clear the
Smiths had stolen the cats to pull off
a bank robbery!

It surprised me that Mr and
Mrs Smith were only robbing a bank
and not planning to take over the
world. Everything about them said
criminal mastermind to me. Then
I turned the paper over and found a
note scribbled in the corner.

'After robbery – steal
more cats and then
TAKE OVER THE
WORLD!'

I knew it!

I also knew from
Mrs Smith's careless

whispering that the job was going down tonight – which didn't leave much time. So I stuffed my rucksack full of gadgets, dressed in black leggings, black jumper and a black

woolly hat, and then shimmied down the drainpipe and headed straight for the high street.

I got to the bank just as Mr and Mrs Smith pulled up in their van.

Diving into a nearby doorway I watched from the shadows as Mrs Smith tiptoed round to the back of the vehicle, flung the rear doors open and clapped her hands together twice. Suddenly dozens of cats spilled from the van and gathered around her feet.

Mrs Smith pulled a piece of
fish from her pocket and whistled
through her fingers. All of the
cats immediately sat bolt upright
and gazed at her intently; then she

whistled again and they formed an
orderly line outside the bank.

The cats had all been trained!

I watched in amazement as the
woman crouched down and began
whistling a series of complicated
commands. Each pair of furry ears

twitched in turn as she gave the
cats their instructions and a small
piece of fish. Then she stood up
and pointed to the bank.
Suddenly all the cats
sprang into action. Some
scaled the drainpipe, others
climbed up to the first floor
windows and a couple of the
smaller ones clambered through
the bank's deposit
box. Each cat found its
own way inside the bank
until there
were none
left on the
pavement
beside Mrs
Smith.

Mr Smith
stayed in the
van the whole
time revving the
engine, meaning
he was obviously the
getaway driver. But that also
meant that once the cats returned,
the Smiths would speed away with all
the cats and the loot!

I decided there was no way
to stop the van without getting
squashed, so I had to somehow
prevent the animals from returning
to the van. And I had to think fast
because the first of the cat-burglars
had already returned – followed by
another, then another . . .

Some of the cats had wads of

money in their
mouths, others
were holding
bags of cash.
A few were
even wearing
diamond tiaras

and matching
necklaces

(and looking very pleased with
themselves)!

Mrs Smith stood among them and seemed to be counting heads.

I rummaged frantically in my rucksack for a gadget that might help me out, something to cause a big diversion or lure the cats away, but there was nothing appropriate.

Then I glanced down at my jumper . . .

Quick as a flash I snagged a thread, pulled a long length of wool from my sleeve and leaped from my hiding place.

'Here, puss-puss!' I shrieked.

Waving my arm in the air I
legged it past a startled Mrs Smith
and through the sea of newly wealthy

cats, twitching and dangling the
thread over their bobbing heads.

As
I'd
hoped
they started
leaping up,
wide-eyed, and
swiping at the
wool with their paws.

I definitely had their attention,
so before Mrs Smith could work
out what was happening I scarpered
down the high street trailing
the wool behind me. The cats
immediately gave chase – leaving

Mrs Smith alone outside the bank
with her mouth hanging open.

Mr Smith honked the horn and
his wife jumped back into the van,
and with a sudden shrieking of tyres
they chased me – and the trail of rich
moggies – down the high street.

Mr Smith was waving his fist in
the air and Mrs Smith was dangling
out of the window clapping and
whistling frantically. Luckily the cats

were more interested in the wool and completely ignored them – but the van was quickly gaining.

I turned into the nearest alleyway and heard the van screech to a halt behind me. Mr and Mrs Smith leaped out and took up the chase on foot. Glancing back I saw they

were now very red-faced, although I wasn't sure if it was from anger or because they were both short and plump and not used to running.

I had to think fast!

With no time to access my rucksack I looked down at my jumper again.

The thread from my right sleeve was still trailing behind me so I set to work unpicking the left one, pulling out great long loops of wool one after the other, and by the time I reached the street I had a big armful of tangled yarn.

I turned the corner and crouched behind the wall.

The cats gathered around my feet tapping the limp thread half-heartedly, when suddenly the panting couple staggered out of the alleyway. I immediately sprang up and threw the great loopy mess of wool over their heads like a big black web.

With the excitement of so much dangling wool the cats went mad again, and started jumping all over the place swiping at anything that moved. They mostly swiped at Mr and Mrs Smith who were trying to snatch the cash.

'Ow!' said Mr Smith.

'Meow!' said the cats.

'Ow!' said Mrs Smith.

'Meow!' said the cats.

In
all the
confusion I
circled the fishy
couple as fast as
I could,
winding wool
around their arms
and legs like a
spider wrapping a fly.
The more their greedy hands grabbed
for the loot, the more entangled they
became.

Eventually I ran out of
wool and there was
nothing left of my
black jumper,
but by this
time

the cat-nappers were just a big black
blob, and so knotted up they couldn't
move an inch.

The cats were still swiping at loose threads dangling from the woolly cocoon when I noticed passers-by were stopping to watch the spectacle – which must have seemed very peculiar.

When you're a secret agent you can't take credit for saving the world all the time, or else you won't be secret anymore. So I pulled my woolly hat down over my face while I worked out what to do next.

Police sirens wailed in the distance, but I couldn't stick around to explain what had happened.

I had to think fast.

Squinting through

the woolly mesh of my hat I
rummaged inside my rucksack again,
desperately looking for a gadget that
might get me out of another sticky
situation.

Instead I laid my hands on the
'LOST CAT' posters and the bank
blueprint!

'Aha!' I said, (and I didn't mean
a non-existent Aha Bird!)

I pulled a loose thread from
the top of the cocoon and attached
the blueprint firmly to the heads of
Mr and Mrs Smith. Then I stuck all
the 'LOST CAT' posters around the
woolly bundle – the police would
definitely need to know who to
phone once they'd de-cashed the
millionaire moggies.

Nodding happily to myself at a case well solved, I pulled on my rucksack and disappeared into the night (in true secret agent style). Although I did bump into a few people on the way because I couldn't really see where I was going.

I managed to sneak back into my room without Mum knowing,

but the next day I got into trouble for 'losing' my black jumper. Although Mum didn't make a big deal about it – I think she was secretly pleased.

In fact Mum was so not-annoyed that she rushed out and bought a bundle of bright-pink wool. Then Gran set to work knitting me a brand new jumper, a proper cheery one for a girl of my age that wouldn't show up the bits.

Which is OK, because I like pink . . . when I'm not busy being a secret agent.

The Case of the Whispering Weeds

'Must you carry that big rucksack everywhere you go, Amelia?' Mum sighed as I climbed into the back seat of the car. 'I really can't imagine what you think you need, we're only popping to the garden centre to fetch plant food for my droopy roses.'

'Just dolls,' I lied, peering over my sunglasses.

Mum rolled her eyes as we drove away and started giving me a lecture about how I was too old to be

playing with dolls, and that perhaps I
should make some real friends.

My rucksack was actually full
of secret-agent equipment, but I
couldn't tell Mum or she'd worry
about me. Saving the world
can be dangerous and Mum
was definitely better
off thinking I was
playing with
dolls.

I was on a secret mission to investigate suspicious activity going on at the garden centre. Sightings of strange creatures – stuff like that. But it was too far away for me to cycle, so every night after school I crept into the garden to sabotage Mum's favourite rose bushes. I'm not proud of it, and I didn't do any real damage, I just had to make sure they looked a bit sad and droopy by the weekend.

You have to think ahead when you're a secret agent.

I thought I was prepared for
anything when we reached the
garden centre, but I hadn't expected
to run into Trudy Hart! Trudy is in
my class and we don't get on at all.

'Isn't that your friend?' Mum
asked when she spotted Trudy
wandering through the leafy aisles
with her dad. Mum must have seen

Trudy and me arguing at the school gates or something and wrongly assumed we were friends.

'No,' I said flatly, 'she's really not.'

'Yoo hoo!' Mum shrieked, grabbing my arm and pulling me over to where Trudy and her dad were arguing over bedding plants. It sounded like Trudy wanted only pink flowers in the garden and was giving him a really hard time about it.

Trudy and I glared at each other while our parents decided we two should go off together to look at flowers, and all meet up at the check out in an hour. Mum was clearly delighted that I'd be spending time with a real person instead of a doll, while Trudy's dad seemed only too pleased to dump her on me.

Parents always think that just because another kid is roughly the same age, you should have no problems being best friends with them. They don't even think about whether you have anything in common or not. Trudy and I have nothing in common. She's really popular at school and I don't have time to be popular because I'm too busy saving the world.

"Bye, then,' I said to Trudy as soon as we were out of sight of our parents.

'Yeah, good riddance!' snapped Trudy.

Reaching the end of the aisle, Trudy went one way and I went the other.

I had an investigation to carry
out, but I couldn't risk Mum and
Trudy seeing me in secret-agent
mode – or interfering while I was
trying to save the world. So I hid
behind a large potted fern and
rummaged inside my rucksack.

I pulled on a big yellow
summer dress over my clothes,
scraped my hair into a frizzy blonde

wig and then crammed
a big floppy sunhat on
top. I could hardly see
through the frizzy
fringe and the
rim of the hat.
I hoped that
meant no one
would recognise
me.

Turning the corner, my disguise
was immediately put to the test as I
ran straight into Mum!

'Why, I have that exact same
dress!' Mum said conversationally.

(It's no wonder
she recognised
it, it was
Mum's dress!)

But I couldn't stand and have a conversation about it or Mum might also recognise her floppy sunhat and realise it was me.

'This old rag?' I shrieked, in my best impression of a posh woman's voice. 'It's hideous, I only ever use it for gardening!' And with that I grabbed the nearest pot plant and barged past Mum like I was the rudest

woman in the world.

'Well, really!' Mum exclaimed,
shaking her head angrily.

I quickly plonked the plant into
a nearby trolley and whizzed off to
the opposite end of the garden centre.
There I set to work looking for clues,
filling the trolley as I went along like
a real shopper would. You have to

blend in when you're carrying out
surveillance – it looks odd if you're
just sneaking around.

I also kept an eye out for Mum
and Trudy!

After half an hour of searching
I still hadn't found anything
suspicious in the garden centre and,
with only the greenhouse section left,
I was beginning to think nothing
dodgy was going on after all.

I made my way slowly through the aisles of greenhouses, feeling bad about making Mum's roses droopy for nothing, when something suddenly shot across my path!

I froze to the spot, tipped my sunglasses and scanned the floor. I hadn't seen exactly what it was because it moved too fast, but it was bigger than a mouse and scuttled in a very strange way like a small dark octopus!

Crouching down I noticed a faint line of soil on the white-tiled floor!

Whatever it was, the

creature had left a trail!

I immediately turned my trolley and set off after it and I was so busy watching the trail 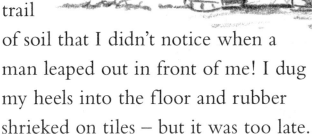 of soil that I didn't notice when a man leaped out in front of me! I dug my heels into the floor and rubber shrieked on tiles – but it was too late.

CRASH!

OOPS!

'Look where you're going, you
silly old fool!' the man growled,
picking himself up from the floor
and patting the dust from his garden-
centre uniform.
He was tall
and thin and
very mean-
looking.

The man
obviously mistook
me for an old lady,

probably because I was hunched over and staring at the floor. So I went along with it and kept my face well hidden beneath the hat.

'Oh! Dearie me!' I croaked. 'I'm terribly sorry, young man.'

'And so you should be!' He snapped. 'There are some very rare plants in this section!' The man shook his fist angrily and then stormed away mumbling under his breath.

I decided it was very strange that the man had been so rude. People who work in shops are supposed to be nice to the customers, even if they mow you down with their trolley. Stranger still was his comment about rare plants. There didn't seem to be any plants at all in this section, just aisles of empty greenhouses.

Hmmm?

I kept an eye out for the strange man and picked up the trail of soil.

Before long the trail stopped dead outside one of the greenhouses. This greenhouse was right at the back of the showroom and was different from the rest. Not only was it bigger and older, but it was also clouded over with condensation so nothing could be seen through the hazy panes of glass.

Leaving the trolley in the aisle, I pushed the glass door

open a fraction and peered inside.
The greenhouse was hot and humid
and full of plants. But they weren't

rare plants – or even
common plants. All
the plants in the
misty greenhouse
looked just like
weeds!
I stepped inside and
glanced around.
None of the plants
were in pots or
bedding trays, so
they were definitely weeds. And they
were scattered all over the floor as if
someone had just weeded out their
garden and dumped them there.

Hmmm?

Reaching inside my rucksack, I pulled out my extendable grabber-hand gadget (which is basically a hand on a stick). Whatever had scuttled across my path must be hiding under the weeds and I didn't want to use my real hand just in case the mysterious creature had teeth!

After a few minutes of careful poking I found nothing among the weeds, but I had to stop to catch my breath. The greenhouse was as hot as an oven and I was baking under the dress, hat and wig.

Realising no one could actually see me through the misted glass of the greenhouse, I peeled off my damp disguise and packed it away. But when I crouched down to refasten my rucksack I

suddenly heard a strange sound coming from the weeds.

To begin with, it sounded like the kind of hissing that grass makes when it's blown by the breeze, but listening carefully it began to sound more and

more like whispering
– as though the weeds
were somehow talking
to each other!

It was then that
I realised something
dreadful.

The creature I'd been
tracking wasn't under the
weeds, the creature was
the weeds. And I was
trapped in a greenhouse

112

with a great big pile of them!

Uh Oh!

The weeds stopped whispering and slowly began to move, roots and leaves gathering around my feet, and some of the more stringy ones were trying to wrap their vines around my shoes!

I jumped back with a gasp.

The weeds immediately started whispering again and spread out on the floor of the greenhouse like a regiment of soldiers. Suddenly they leaped up onto their roots like little

white legs and scuttled after me
waving their leaves angrily in the air.

'*ARRRRRGGGGHHH!*' I
screamed, which admittedly isn't the
sort of thing you're supposed to do
when you're a secret agent, but they

were really creepy and they took me
by surprise.

I threw the door open and was
about to scarper when I saw a tall,
thin figure blocking my path!
It was the man I'd knocked over
with my trolley, and he was smiling
at me.

But it wasn't a
friendly smile – it was
an I'm-going-to-rule-
the-world smile. I've
seen it loads of times
before, criminal
masterminds and
evil geniuses
always have an
I'm-going-to-
rule-the-world smile.

'So you found my
rare plants?' he
chuckled.
I glanced
behind me
at the weeds.
They were
still standing

on their roots but they'd stopped
scuttling. They seemed to be looking
up at the man as if waiting for his
instructions.

The best thing to do when
confronted by a criminal mastermind
or an evil genius is to keep cool
and not let them know
you're scared. It was
difficult, especially
knowing the

whispering weeds were right behind
me, but I gave the man my best

fearless glare.

'You won't get away with this!'
I growled, and waved my extendable
grabber-hand at him.

'Won't get away with what?'
asked the man, frowning at my
gadget.

'With . . . whatever it is you're
trying to get away with!' I said,
realising I still wasn't sure exactly
what the man was up to with his
creepy weed-army. But I was fully
expecting a big long rant about
taking over the world – that's
what criminal masterminds
and evil
geniuses
always do.
'You're

too late, little girl!' the thin man said. 'My troops are ready! Once dispatched they will creep into every garden and spread into every field and farm in the world . . .'

If evil geniuses and criminal masterminds didn't spend so much time ranting about their plans to take over the world, they'd probably be a lot more successful. But they love bragging about how clever they are – so I used the time to look for a way to stop him. My eyes fell on my shopping trolley sitting in the aisle behind him.

'. . . my weed army will control every crop on the planet!' he continued. 'Then I will hold the whole world to ransom!'

With one careful flick of my grabber-hand I extended it behind the man and into the trolley. Then, grabbing a big terracotta pot, I flicked it up in the air and dropped it on his head.

'*OW!*' The man growled, rubbing the top of his head angrily.

It didn't knock him out but he was distracted long enough for me to shoot past.

I grabbed the handle of the trolley and ran as fast as I could. The trolley had filled up quite a bit while I was pretending to be a shopper, so it quickly picked up speed. Once it was going fast enough I leaped into

the basket and rode it through the
aisles of greenhouses.

Looking back, I saw the man
stoop down to whisper to the weed
army gathered at his feet, then he
nodded in my direction and the
weeds suddenly started chasing me!

They shot across the floor
hissing and waving their
leaves.

Rummaging
inside the trolley
for stuff to
throw
at them,
I laid my
hands on two
green

spray bottles. I lifted them out and
was about to lob them at the gaining
vegetation when I caught sight of the
labels.

SUPER STRONG
WEED KILLER!

Squirt!

Squirt!

I quickly
flicked the caps
off the bottles with my
thumbs, curled my fingers
round the plastic triggers and, as the
first of the weeds leaped into the air,
I squirted them!

They instantly fell away,
landing with a splat, but the others
kept on coming.

Squirt! Squirt! Squirt!

As the last angry weed splatted
on the floor in a limp mushy heap,

Squirt!

Squirt!

I looked back at the thin man.
Needless to say, he'd lost his I'm-
going-to-rule-the-world smile. It
was now replaced with the equally
familiar my-life's-work-is-ruined
grimace!

He wouldn't be causing any trouble in a hurry!

I was about to feel pleased with myself for saving the world again, when I suddenly realised I was still sitting in a trolley moving at very high speed through aisles of greenhouses.

Uh Oh!

I leaped off the trolley and grabbed the handle. Digging my heels into the floor, I managed to steer to avoid one crash, only to send the trolley hurtling round the corner and into the main section of the garden centre!

Still
holding on,
the trolley dragged
me through the leafy aisles
when suddenly I heard a thud and a
very startled '*Yelp!*'

I peered over the top of the handle and saw a very dazed Trudy sitting in the trolley with her arms and legs hanging over the sides. Picking up an unexpected passenger definitely slowed the trolley down but peering through Trudy's legs I saw something up ahead – something we were heading straight for.

It was the check-out till, and standing beside it was Mum and Trudy's dad.

They both looked up at the same time and their mouths fell open.

CRASH!

OOPS!

On the way home in the car Mum was silent. She usually gives me the 'silent treatment' when she's really angry. It happens quite a lot because saving the world often gets me into trouble.

In fact Mum only spoke once during the whole trip home.

'That girl Trudy is clearly a very bad influence on you and I don't want to see you hanging around with her again,' Mum growled, shaking her head at the memory of Trudy and me crashing into the check-out till and overturning the trolley.

'OK,' I said, thinking this was a bit of a bonus.

'And on second thoughts,' Mum added, glancing back at my bulging rucksack, 'perhaps you *are* better off playing with your dolls, they're definitely a lot less dangerous!'

The Case of the Zombie Cows

During the holidays, when Mum's not working, we go out for the day and usually try to go to a different place each time. More often than not we end up somewhere really cool, but then other times we end up somewhere not so cool.

This time Mum decided on the local petting zoo. Which is cool if you're really young – but not so cool if you're a secret agent who has definitely grown out of fluffy bunny rabbits.

I admit I was in a bit of a sulk when we arrived, huffing and puffing as we made our way down the gravel path towards the farmyard. Unfortunately Mum saw this as an opportunity for a bit of interrogation.

'Amelia, why oh why do you insist on dragging that big heavy bag everywhere we go?' she said, jabbing a finger at my rucksack. 'I can't imagine what you think you'll need?'

'Stuff,' I said, eyeing her carefully over the top of my sunglasses.

Mum eyed me carefully back.

Sometimes saying 'stuff' will cover it and Mum won't bother to pursue the contents of my rucksack. But my mum is pretty smart and every so often curiosity gets the better of her.

'What kind of stuff exactly?' she asked.

'Drawing stuff,' I said innocently.

'So I can draw the
fluffy bunny
rabbits.'

Mum immediately raised a
suspicious eyebrow. I'd obviously gone
too far with the mention of fluffy
bunny rabbits; now I was going
to have to prove it or bring
unwanted attention to my
secret-agent activities.

With the biggest sigh I could manage I heaved off my rucksack, unzipped the flap, pulled out a drawing book and a handful of pencils, and waved them in the air. Of course the rest of my bag was stuffed with secret agent stuff.

But in the last week I'd seen Mum grow increasingly inquisitive about my rucksack, and

had packed the book and
pencils as a precaution.

You have
to think ahead
when you're a
secret agent.

'I don't want to see them,' Mum
shrugged innocently. 'I was just
making conversation.'

As I suspected, the petting zoo wasn't
very interesting.

The animals were cute but they were all small and fluffy, and I couldn't really see them anyway because there were lots of other kids crowding around – kids that were at least half my age!

To make matters worse Mum
bumped into an old friend and was
nattering for ages, so I sloped away to
look for some bigger, more grown-up
animals like horses or elephants. OK I
didn't really expect to find an
elephant, but it was a farm so there
could be a horse.

I was in luck –
as soon as I
turned the
corner,

climbed a couple of fences and
negotiated my way through a hedge, I
eventually found the stables. But my
luck quickly ran out as
very loud voice stopped
me in my tracks.

'AMELIA KIDD!
WHAT ON EARTH
ARE *YOU* DOING
HERE?'

At first I thought Mum had seen
me sneaking off, followed me and
planned to march me
back to the fluffy
bunny rabbits.
But then I realised
the voice was much
too high-pitched
and whiny –
which could
mean only one
other person.

I turned round
slowly to see Trudy
Hart storming across
the courtyard in riding
coat, boots and
hat, waving her
crop at me.

Trudy is in my class at school
and we don't get on, in fact we're
sworn enemies.

'Well?' she demanded, eyeing me
up and down with her nose high in
the air.

Because she took me by
surprise, I was about to explain that I
was bored with the petting zoo and

was looking for something more interesting to pet, but then I thought of a better response.

'It's none of your business!' I yelled.

'My daddy owns these stables so I think you'll find it is my business!' she snapped.

'Oh,' I said, lowering my voice and forcing my mouth into a fake smile. 'I wasn't doing any harm, I just wanted to see the horses.'

'They're not *rocking* horses, they're intelligent animals and I forbid you from going anywhere near them!'

Trudy sneered, and thrust her riding crop in the direction of a nearby field.

'I will allow you to see the cows, though, they're awfully stupid so you'll probably find you have a lot in common!'

I was about to raise my voice again when a short, thin man appeared from one of the stables. My secret agent senses immediately kicked in when I noticed the man was carrying a shiny black briefcase!

Evil geniuses and criminal masterminds often carry briefcases to hold their fiendish plans for world domination. That doesn't mean *everyone* who has a  briefcase is planning to take over the world, but this man was obviously just a stable hand, which made it *very* suspicious.

'Lightning is ready for you, Miss Trudy,' he said.

The man caught me peering at
him over my sunglasses and narrowed
his eyes, making him look like an
angry gnome. 'Is everything OK, Miss
Trudy?' he added cautiously.

'Yes, thank you, Albert,' said
Trudy, without looking round. 'It's just
one of those dreadful petting-zoo
people who's got lost again, but I said
she could go and gawp at the cows.'

'But the cows aren't really part of—' Albert began, but Trudy cut him off.

'I *said* she could go and gawp at the cows,' Trudy repeated – pulling out her mobile phone and flicking it open in a threatening manner. 'Is there going to be a problem, Albert?'

'No, miss,' he said hurriedly. 'No problem at all.'

Trudy snapped her phone shut and grinned at me.

'Off you go then,' she said, 'and if I catch you near the stables again, I'll have Albert run you off with his pitchfork. Do you understand?'

I wasn't listening anymore, I was watching Albert shuffling away and looking very dodgy. Once he was out of sight I turned my attention back to Trudy; she was snorting through her nostrils at being made to wait.

'Whatever,' I sighed, and casually strolled away.

I made my way towards the cow field and then hid behind the wall until Trudy finally trotted off on her horse. I planned to double back and carry out some stable surveillance – but first I needed a disguise.

Ducking into the empty cattle
shed I rummaged through
my rucksack.

Making room for the
sketchbook and
pencil decoy meant
disguises were thin
on the ground, so I
had to make do with a
plastic nose, moustache

and glasses (all in one), and a flat cap. A glance in my compact mirror told me none of my flowery dresses would go with the moustache,  but after a bit of snooping I found an old brown coat hanging in the shed.

Pulling the coat on over my rucksack to give myself a bit of a hunch, I stepped back into the yard and glanced around. I was about to head back for the stables when I heard a very strange sound coming from the field.

MOO-click-click!

MOO-click-click!

A small herd of cows were ambling awkwardly towards me, but there was something very odd about the way they moved, something creepy and clunky, like zombie cows.

The cows stopped suddenly when they reached the fence and peered at me through vacant eyes. I'd never seen a cow up close before but I was pretty sure they didn't tick – and these cows were definitely ticking!

At first I thought they might be time bombs made to look like cows, but that didn't really make sense. So I stood up on the fence, leaned over and tapped one firmly on the head. It was rock hard and echoed like a tin drum, and on closer inspection I found that one of the ears was not an ear at all but a large metal key!

Slipping through the fence I gave the cow a quick once-over.

After a bit of expert tapping and knocking and banging, a small door clicked open in the cow's belly. Peering inside the hatch I found a mass of cogs and wheels and ratchets whirring around, which definitely explained the ticking.

The cow was made of clockwork!

Slamming the hatch I suddenly
noticed that none of the clockwork
cows actually had a tail, instead they
each had a radio-control antenna with
a tiny red beacon flashing at the end!

'*Hmmm?*' I thought to myself.

An antenna meant they were
not just clockwork cattle that roamed
the fields until their keys wound

down, which would be weird enough; these cows were actually being controlled by someone from a distance!

Slowly and discreetly I pulled out my compact mirror, held it up and scanned the scene behind me, and there in the stable courtyard was Albert the shifty stable hand! He was watching me closely while tapping away frantically inside his briefcase.

Suddenly all the cows clicked their heads in my direction.

'*MOOOOO!*' they boomed together, and then started making their way forward again. Dropping the mirror, I leaped back over the fence just as the cows crashed through it!

In the courtyard Albert had vanished round the back of the stables, so I ran after him as fast as my disguise would allow – which was faster than the cows, who were very slow and ambled along like zombies.

Tucked away behind the stables I found a chicken run and Albert was standing behind the hutch with his briefcase propped up against the roof.

I could now see that
it had an antenna
of its own
and was full
of dials and
buttons and
switches.

When he
saw me he gave
an evil-genius smile and prodded one
of the buttons dramatically.

Cluck-click-click!

Cluck-click-click!

With a whirring of tiny cogs
and wheels and ratchets every chicken
in the yard stopped acting like a
chicken, and snapped
its head in my
direction.

They flapped their
wings angrily and
began bobbing up
and down like
demented pistons.

Glancing back around the stable
I could see the herd of cows were still
bumbling across the courtyard. It
wasn't exactly a stampede so I turned
my attention back to the chickens.

The bobbing seemed to be
powering up the springs in their legs
because one tin bird squatted down, a
click sounded, and then it launched
itself straight at me, snapping its beak
angrily.

Uh Oh!

Quick as a flash I grabbed a nearby shovel and volleyed the ball of flapping metal before it could peck my plastic nose off.

I'm quite good at tennis so it shot across the yard like a rocket, landing with a massive

CLANG!

The pecking projectiles whizzed
through the air in rapid succession
and I fended them off with my shovel.
As the last of the clockwork chickens
squatted, clicked and launched, I
turned sideways and whacked it in the
direction of a very angry Albert.

The tin torpedo sailed through
the air and crashed
into the briefcase,
knocking Albert
off his feet.

The controls slid
down the roof of
the chicken coop
and Albert lunged
forward, but I was
quicker and
managed to
snatch it in
midair.

'Give
that back!'
Albert
growled,
getting to
his feet
and dusting
himself off.

I knew Albert was short, but he
was a lot shorter than I'd realised.

In fact he was so short that I could keep the briefcase from his reach just by holding it up in the air. Albert looked even more like an angry gnome jumping up and down trying to grab the briefcase.

Eventually the little man tired himself out.

'Now, why don't you start by telling me what you're up to?' I demanded, and because I was taller I felt like a grown-up dealing with a naughty child.

'Are you planning to take over the world?'

'Uh?' said Albert, and seemed genuinely surprised. 'Of course not...'

'Then what?' I said, stepping back and peering inside the briefcase.

'I'm planning to take over the *horse racing* world!' he stated proudly.

'On a metal chicken?' I said, and then glanced back at the cows, who were now ambling around the corner and looking much more comical than scary. 'Or on one of those?' I added with a smirk.

'Oh, those are just experiments,' Albert said, shaking his head. 'Now I've perfected my mechanical-animal technology there isn't be a single horse that can beat Lightning.'

'Lightning?' I gasped. 'Trudy Hart's horse?'

'Lightning belongs to me!' snapped Albert. 'That little madam thinks she owns everything just because her father owns the stables, but he's mine – I made every cog and spring.'

'Lightning isn't even a real

horse?' I said, and was a little bit impressed.

'No, in fact he's *better* than a real horse!' said Albert matter-of-factly.

Hearing the familiar *tick-tick-ticking*, I noticed that the herd had eventually caught up with me, so I scanned the control board inside the briefcase for the stop button.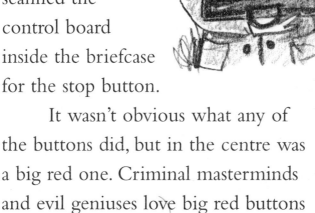

It wasn't obvious what any of the buttons did, but in the centre was a big red one. Criminal masterminds and evil geniuses love big red buttons

in briefcases —
they usually mean
something bad like
an explosion or
an ejector seat
or something
like that.

But seeing as Albert wasn't technically
trying to take over the world, I
guessed that the big red button just
meant 'stop'.

So I pressed it.

That was when lots of things
happened all at once.

Albert leaped
forward yelling,

'NOOOOOOOOO!'

The slow stampede of clockwork cows ground to a halt and then each one exploded in a mass of springs and cogs and little brass wheels.

Moments later there was a very loud shriek. It came from the courtyard on the other side of the

stables and, even in all the chaos, I knew it belonged to Trudy Hart, because I've heard her shrieking loads of times before.

'What have you done?' Albert groaned, snatching the smoking briefcase and clutching it to his chest.

'Er, I'm not sure,' I said awkwardly. 'What *have* I done?'

'That was the self-destruct button,' Albert sobbed, sinking helplessly to his knees. 'It's linked to *all* the mechanical animals and was there only for an emergency, it was never supposed to be pressed!'

'Oh,' I said feebly. 'Sorry.'

I did feel bad for breaking Albert's animals, but then I decided it was probably best to put an end to his plot. If he'd succeeded in taking over the racing world, he would most likely have turned his attention to the rest of the world.

It's best to nip these things in the bud.

Leaving Albert with his briefcase,

I decided to make my way back towards the petting zoo. Packing my disguise away, I draped the brown coat over the fence and stepped back through the stables.

In the middle of the courtyard sat a heap of clockwork, springs and metal horse parts. In the middle of the mechanical mess sat Trudy. She was still perched in the saddle holding onto the reins, angrily tapping the hide with her riding crop.

'Giddy up!' she demanded, as the metal torso creaked back and forth.

'Nice rocking horse,' I said, slipping my sunglasses on with a smile.

The Case of the Perilous Pipe

'. . . So if you think about it, another
day really won't make any difference,'
I pleaded, standing outside the school
gates with my hands
clasped hopefully.
'I'm already a
week behind.'

    'And that's
exactly why you need
to go back today,'
Mum said sternly.

'Your cold has gone and your temperature is back to normal, so there's really no reason to keep you away from school a moment longer.'

I coughed dramatically but Mum just rolled her eyes.

'Have a nice day!' she said, jumped back into the car and drove away.

I do like school, but I'd got used to sitting in bed watching TV and being waited on by Mum. It was also nice to have a break from being a secret agent and saving the world. I consoled myself with the fact that my first lesson of the day was music – something nice and relaxing to ease me back in.

Or so I thought!

In the week I'd been away our old music teacher had retired and had been replaced by someone called Mrs Piper. In my experience new teachers always spell trouble; they're usually quite clever and therefore prone to thoughts of world domination.

Admittedly the dodgy ones are mostly chemistry teachers or biology teachers, but even the odd maths teacher can be found calculating mathematical formulas to take over the world.

I'd never actually heard of a music teacher being a criminal mastermind or an evil genius, but I decided to keep an eye on Mrs Piper just in case.

In class, I peered over my sunglasses as the new music teacher took off her coat and arranged books on her desk, which wasn't at all suspicious.

Then, after calling the
register, she frowned
and ran her finger back
down the list of names.

'Amelia Kidd?'
she said, narrowing
her eyes.

'Here!' I said,
just in case she
was calling
the register
again.

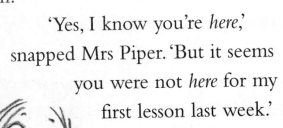

'Yes, I know you're *here*,'
snapped Mrs Piper. 'But it seems
you were not *here* for my
first lesson last week.'

'I was sick,' I
said. 'But I'm pretty
sure I'll catch up.'

'I'm absolutely certain you will catch up!' said Mrs Piper firmly, 'because when you return to this classroom at lunch time I will repeat the entire lesson to ensure you catch up!'

'Er . . .' I said, but she cut me off before I could come up with a decent excuse.

'Now, who can remind me of the wonderful tune we learned last week?' Mrs Piper demanded, closing the register and turning her attention to the rest of the class.

Every hand shot into the air and waved enthusiastically.

'Good,' she said, placing a long black case on her desk, flicking the clasp and pulling out a funny-looking recorder. 'Then you will have no trouble accompanying me on my medieval pipe.'

Mrs Piper played three notes and the class sang, '*La! La! La!*'

Not knowing the tune or the point of the lesson, all I could do was watch and listen, which was much more difficult than it sounds. The class sang the same three notes over and over again like a broken record and the sound of the weird wooden instrument made my brain itch.

With each chorus of '*La! La! La!*' my secret agent instincts told me something strange was going on in the classroom, but I couldn't put my finger on exactly what it was.

'La! La! La!'

For one thing everyone was very enthusiastic about the 'La! La! La!' No one was fidgeting or getting bored. Also, everyone sang exactly in time with the pipe which never happens with a bunch of kids singing together – unless they're in a choir, and even then...

I turned my attention to Mrs Piper, purse-lipped and shifting her fingers swiftly along the pipe. Then I looked at the instrument itself, which was intricately carved and looked very old, meaning it was probably an antique . . .

An antique!

'*Aha!*' I thought, because in my experience antiques are always trouble: whether they're cursed or enchanted or have spirits trapped in them, you can't trust antiques.

But could the whole class really be under the influence of the pipe?

The '*La! La! La!*' ended abruptly and every head turned in my direction.

'Amelia Kidd!' snapped the teacher. 'Will you be joining in or do you plan to continue gazing around the room like a gormless frog?'

Being a secret agent means you have to think fast, and my fast thoughts told me I could now find out for certain if the class was under the influence of the strange antique pipe.

I glanced over to Trudy Hart.

Having just been singled out by the teacher and called a gormless frog, I knew Trudy couldn't resist a sneer or a snigger.

Trudy looked back and gave me a friendly smile, but it wasn't a sarcastic friendly smile, it was a genuine friendly smile that made the hairs on the back

of my neck stand
on end.

The class were
definitely under the
influence of the pipe!

Mrs Piper
played the same
tune once again and
the whole class sang it back
with perfect timing. She gave a
satisfied nod and then turned to me
with a raised eyebrow.

'*La? La? La?*' I
mumbled, uncertainly.

Mrs Piper
nodded again and was
about to resume playing
when the bell for
break time sounded.

Immediately the whole class began shifting and fidgeting in their chairs. It seemed the bell had broken the trance, and for confirmation of this I turned to Trudy Hart.

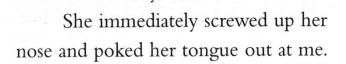

She immediately screwed up her nose and poked her tongue out at me.

At break time I was sitting on a bench, trying to work out how to get a closer look at Mrs Piper's peculiar pipe, when the din from the playground was suddenly replaced by an eerie silence.

I looked around over my sunglasses.

All the kids had mysteriously stopped playing, running and screaming and stood perfectly still like statues. Then I heard a familiar tune coming from the window of the music room and saw the silhouette of Mrs Piper and her pipe.

'La! La! La!'   'La! La! La!'

Singing the song of the distant pipe, the whole playground turned to face me and began walking in my direction, and not just the kids from my music class, it was every kid in the school.

Everyone except me was under Mrs Piper's spell!

Realising the music teacher was on to me I grabbed my rucksack and was about to leg it when another sound echoed through the playground – the bell signalling the end of break time.

All the kids
stopped, looked
around and began
scratching their
heads.

The bell had broken the spell
again, but it was too close for comfort.
Pulling on my rucksack, I hurried back
into school and ran straight to the next
class on my timetable.

It was computer studies, and I
had some research to do!

After a
week away from
school, I knew
I'd be a bit
behind on
most of my
subjects, but
computer
studies wasn't one
of them. Secret agents have to be
super quick on computers so I'm
always ahead of everyone else – and I
planned to use that time to find out
about medieval pipes and the
mysterious Mrs Piper.

It took me a while, but after a
lot of digging I found a picture of
Mrs Piper's pipe. It was called the
Perilous Pipe and loads of historical

documents mentioned it. As I suspected the instrument was enchanted, which means a spell had been cast on it back in the days when people cast spells.

The Perilous Pipe had been enchanted nearly three hundred years ago – or rather the reed that makes the sound *inside* the pipe had been enchanted – but what was interesting was that it had originally belonged to someone called The Piper!

Which was all a bit too much of a coincidence if you ask me.

I made another search.

There were lots of different references to The Piper, some were stories and others were real historical accounts from old newspapers and journals. The one thing they all had in common was what The Piper was famous for.

He was famous for leading children away using the Perilous Pipe!

I even found an old-fashioned drawing of The Piper and the resemblance made me gasp out loud.

I glanced up from the screen to make sure no one had heard me and I was just in time to see Mrs Piper creeping past the window with a large pair of bolt cutters!

This made me gasp even louder!

'Amelia?' said Mr Moore. 'Are you feeling well?'

The tech teacher looked concerned and started weaving through the computer desks towards me.

Thinking fast I quickly cleared the
screen and pulled a big wad of tissues
out of my rucksack.
I wiped my
nose and peered
helplessly up
at him.

'Just a few sniffles!' I sighed,
glancing sideways at the clock.

It was ten minutes to lunch time
and I decided I could use those ten
minutes to snoop around Mrs Piper's

classroom. Taking a deep breath I launched an enormous coughing fit into my tissues.

'Oh dear!' said Mr Moore. 'I think you should take yourself along to see the nurse immediately.'

Pulling on my rucksack I nodded bravely and headed for the door, throwing in a couple of sniffs for good measure. Once out of sight I pocketed the tissues and bolted.

Backing along the wall of the corridor I peered through the door of the music room – there were no lessons going on inside but Mrs Piper had already returned. She was standing at the window looking out into the playground where I'd seen her at break time.

On her desk lay the Perilous Pipe.

This was my chance!

Opening the door quietly, I crept into the classroom and tiptoed towards the desk, but I'd only made it halfway before Mrs Piper spoke, and because it startled me I froze to the spot.

'The mark of a truly gifted musician is excellent hearing,' said Mrs Piper, turning round dramatically and glancing at her watch. 'You're early!'

I smiled innocently and shrugged.

Mrs Piper narrowed her eyes.

'Why are you early?' she added suspiciously.

Our eyes met over the Perilous Pipe and as the expression on Mrs Piper's face changed I realised she'd rumbled me. We both ran for the pipe at the same time, but as Mrs Piper was much taller, I knew she'd get there first.

I reached into my pocket, hoping I'd left a small gadget there or something I could use to even the odds, but what I found was the wad of paper tissues.

Not ideal, but I threw them at her anyway.

'*URRRRGGGH!*' she shrieked, batting the air angrily as the tissue-storm surrounded her – the tissues were actually clean, but Mrs Piper didn't know that. I quickly scrabbled onto the desk and searched for the pipe, but as the last of the tissues fluttered down I saw that it was gone.

'Looking for this?' smiled Mrs Piper, waving the weird wooden instrument in the air triumphantly.

'You won't get away with it!' I said angrily.

'Oh, don't bother trying to get me to rant about my plans,' she said dismissively. 'I'm going to steal all the children away with my pipe and then hold the world to ransom. It's that simple really.'

I'd never met an evil genius or a criminal mastermind that didn't like ranting about their evil plans, so this took me by surprise.

The taking-over-the-world rant usually gives me time to come up with a strategy, but Mrs Piper didn't hang around.

She lifted the pipe to her lips and began playing.

I still hadn't been brainwashed by the tune, but as the sound filtered out of the classroom I heard chairs scraping across the floor all over the school, followed by the sound of footsteps marching towards the music room.

Soon the corridor outside filled with kids and Trudy Hart was right at the front wearing that creepy friendly smile.

My only chance for escape was the lunch-time bell breaking the spell. I looked at the clock and saw more than ten minutes had passed since leaving the computer room.

The bell should have sounded already!

'Ring! Ring! It's lunch time!' sang Mrs Piper. 'And now I think it's time for you to catch up with the rest of your class,' she added, shifting her fingers along the pipe and pursing her lips.

Now I knew what Mrs Piper had been doing with the bolt cutters! Seeing the flaw in her plan at break time she'd crept around the school and disconnected all the bells.

I looked around frantically for an escape route, but the kids were blocking the door and the windows were too high up. I tried to remember our last fire drill and whether there was an emergency exit somewhere nearby . . .

Fire drill! I thought, tipping my sunglasses and smiling at Mrs Piper.

My smile obviously took her by surprise because she paused for a moment, and in that moment I snatched the Perilous Pipe, whacked it against the fire alarm and legged it for the door.

As the sound of the fire bells filled the corridor, the kids began scratching their heads, and as I barged past Trudy I was relieved to see her poking her tongue out at me.

Confused teachers were flapping their arms amid the sea of equally confused kids, trying to organise everyone for the fire drill and, in all the chaos, no one noticed as I ducked down and rummaged in my rucksack.

Tucking my hair up inside a baseball cap, I quickly blended back into the crowd as we were led outside to form orderly lines.

I kept my head down and the pipe behind my back as Mrs Piper stalked the lines of kids – and she walked straight past me twice thinking I was just one of many boys in baseball caps.

When the fire alarm was re-set
the teachers spread out and began
calling the registers. Peering under the
peak of my cap I saw Mrs Piper
abandon her search and smile to
herself as the names were called.

As 'K' for 'Kidd' drew nearer on
the register I wracked my brains,
thinking about the research and the
stories and the enchantment . . . *Aha!*
I thought, blindly fiddling with the
pipe behind my back.

'Amelia
Kidd?' called
Mr Moore.

'Here!' I said, slipping off the baseball cap.

Mrs Piper leaped forward, shoved Mr Moore out of the way and snatched the pipe from behind my back.

'You fool!' she yelled, jabbing the antique instrument in my direction like a duelling sword. 'You thought you could prevent *me* from taking over the world?'

'Excuse me?' said Mr Moore, frowning at Mrs Piper.

'Yes, you heard me correctly,' snapped the music teacher. 'I plan to take over the world. It is a genius plan involving my enchanted pipe . . .'

It seemed Mrs Piper couldn't resist a rant after all, and she ranted on and on and on, revealing every aspect of her plot for world domination.

It was actually one of the longest rants I've ever heard from an evil genius or criminal mastermind.

Of course everyone was looking at Mrs Piper as though she'd gone mad, especially when she lifted the pipe to her lips, positioned her hands over the appropriate holes and blew... and no sound came out.

There was a scuffle when Mrs Piper lunged for me, but she was quickly restrained and taken away, yelling about interfering little hooligans, and magical pipes, and stolen enchanted reeds.

A few kids giggled and the teachers shook their heads sadly.

When Mum picked me up she asked if I'd missed anything interesting during my week off sick. Pulling the enchanted reed from my back pocket, I tipped my glasses and studied it closely. It was obviously harmless without the pipe so I snapped it in half, and flicked the pieces out of the window.

'Not really,' I said, smiling to myself. 'But it's definitely good to be back.'

The Case of the Creepy Cakes

On Saturdays Mum takes me to the cake shop around the corner and we treat ourselves to a jam doughnut or a fresh-cream cake. We've done it for as long as I can remember and I always look forward to it.

Or at least I *used* to look forward to it . . .

In the week since our last visit the cake shop had mysteriously closed down and re-opened calling itself 'The Beauty Sisters' Cake Emporium', which is a bit of a flashy name for a cake shop if you ask me.

But the shop wasn't the only thing that was different.

'Look at the size of those doughnuts!' Mum squealed as we passed the window of the shop.

'They must be twice the size of the old ones, and they're half the price too!' she gasped.

I tipped my glasses and peered at the selection of cakes.

It was true, the doughnuts were massive – in fact all the cakes in the window were freakishly huge. There were enormous éclairs, colossal cream horns, mammoth meringues – and all at half the regular price.

My first instinct was to get excited like Mum had, but then my secret agent instincts kicked in and I viewed the outsized cakes with suspicion. I wanted to know why the cakes were so big, why they were so cheap, and who were the strangely generous Beauty Sisters?

Because evil
geniuses and criminal
masterminds don't
usually hang out in
cake shops, I hadn't
brought my rucksack
full of gadgets. But I

still had my sunglasses, so I adjusted
them carefully to conceal my identity
and slipped discreetly into the shop.

Any hope of going unnoticed while carrying out preliminary surveillance was foiled when Mum entered the shop behind me clapping her hands together loudly.

'I THINK I'VE JUST DIED AND GONE TO HEAVEN!' she shrieked, gazing with wide eyes at wall-to-wall shelves stuffed with every confection known to man.

Behind the counter, the heads of two thin figures snapped in our direction. For a fraction of a second the elderly pair narrowed their eyes, but then they quickly stretched their mouths into wide friendly smiles.

'Welcome to The Beauty Sisters' Cake Emporium!' they sang, ignoring me to focus their greeting on Mum.

Which was handy, because now I had a chance to size them up without drawing attention to myself.

The first remarkable thing about the Beauty Sisters was that they were identical twins. Everything about them was a mirror image and probably had been for about a hundred years because they both looked ancient.

The second remarkable thing was how they were dressed.

As they stepped out from behind the counter the pair were both unbelievably glamorous – but it wasn't the usual funky-grandma kind of glamour. This was full-on catwalk glamour, complete with mad clothes, huge hairdos and tonnes of bright make-up.

Mum's wide eyes grew a little wider when confronted with the Beauty Sisters, so much so that for a moment she seemed unable to speak.

'Goodness me,' she gasped eventually. 'You're both, er…'

'Beautiful?' the sisters chimed together. 'Yes, we know.'

'Um, yes!' Mum stammered. 'That's exactly what I was about to say!'

'We used to be supermodels, you know,' the pair stated proudly.

While the grown-ups made small talk, I scanned the shop for signs of criminal activity. But aside from the size of the cakes there was nothing out of the ordinary, except for the peculiar-looking twins.

'. . . and however do you both stay so slim?' Mum laughed. 'If I had a shop like this I'd be tempted to eat cakes all day long,' she added, and then laughed some more.

The twins were not laughing at Mum's joke. In fact they'd stopped smiling altogether and their identical faces suddenly wore the same grave expression.

'We *never* eat the cakes,' they hissed, and with that the sisters

hurried back behind the counter and
busied themselves behind a display of
giant French Fancies.

'Oh,' said Mum, to fill the
awkward silence.

While Mum tried to work out
what she'd said wrong, I crept over
to the counter. Tipping my sunglasses,

I watched as the angry twins
whispered to each other while
frantically tying pink bows around
bags of marzipan sweets.

Suddenly two pairs of eyes
glared in my direction.

'What do you want, little girl?'
they said in unison.

'Two doughnuts, please!' I said,
and did my best innocent smile.

Back home
I eyed the bag of
doughnuts on the
kitchen counter.
They did look and
smell delicious, but
I didn't plan on
Mum or me
eating them. The

Beauty Sisters were up to something –
probably trying to take over the world
– and I was certain the cakes were at
the bottom of it.

I studied the contents of the
paper bag and wondered what an evil
genius or a criminal mastermind
could possibly do with a doughnut,
and the answer seemed pretty obvious
to me.

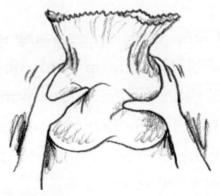

Holding the bag at arm's length I gripped each doughy ball through the paper and began a slow, controlled squeeze. Then, with my face still screwed up because I half-expected the doughnuts to explode, I peered into the bag and was a bit disappointed to see two saggy doughnuts and a bag full of jam.

Hmmm?

I dipped my finger in the sticky red goo and held it up to my nose. It smelled OK but I still didn't want to eat it. Instead, I pulled out my magnifying glass and moved to the window for a closer look.

It was then that something strange happened: as the heat from the sun intensified through the magnifying glass, the jam started bubbling and expanding right before my eyes!

'Heat!' I gasped.

I flicked the red blob away, grabbed the doughnut bag and plonked it on the hot radiator. The jam in the bag immediately began to swell. It strained at the paper and then rose up out of the top like a soufflé. Thinking fast I ran to the bin and threw the whole thing in just as the paper burst and spilled the red mess everywhere.

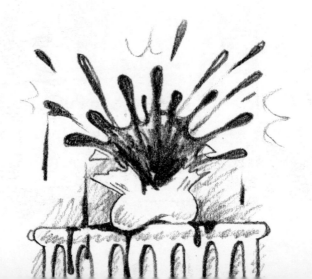

'What on earth?' yelled Mum, appearing in the doorway.

'Er, I dropped our doughnuts in the bin . . . accidentally,' I stammered, although given more time I would definitely have come up with a better excuse.

Mum gazed at the red mess in the bin.

'And they look like really jammy ones too,' she sighed.

'I'll run back to the shop!' I said quickly. 'My treat!' And before Mum could answer I grabbed my rucksack and bolted for the door. Round the corner, I stopped and had a rummage. Without time to prepare, I wasn't sure what disguises I'd packed and all I could find was a beret and a flowery scarf that I'd collected because I might need to look like a French lady one day.

It was not ideal, but it would have to do.

Walking slowly past the window of the cake shop I spied the Beauty Sisters. They were busy talking to customers at the counter so I seized the opportunity to slip into the shop. Once inside, I edged my way discreetly along the wall pretending to browse the shelves, while secretly heading for the curtain at the back.

With one last glance to make sure the twins were still distracted, I was about to duck through the curtain when a terrifying noise stopped me in my tracks.

'BUT I WANT IT NOOOOOW!' screamed a strangely familiar voice.

I froze to the spot.

Pulling my beret down and my scarf up, I slowly turned my head again to find the customers in the shop were actually my archenemy Trudy Hart, and her weary-looking parents.

Trudy is in my class at school but we don't get on. She's very spoiled and used to getting her own way. Today that meant screaming and stamping her foot in the middle of the shop while her parents tried to calm her down.

Typical! I thought.

Then I realised that with Trudy in a full-on tantrum, everyone's attention was focused on her and no one was looking at me. So I shrugged my shoulders and stepped casually through the curtain.

I'd never seen the back of a cake shop before so I didn't really know what to expect, but I definitely didn't expect to find what I found. The back of The Beauty Sisters' Cake Emporium looked exactly like a mad scientist's laboratory!

There were test tubes and lightning rods and smoking beakers, and among all the complicated

scientific equipment were bags of sugar, sacks of flour, pots of cream and jars of jam. There was also a light frost covering everything because the room was as cold as a freezer.

Hmmm? I thought, rubbing my arms for warmth.

My plan to get into the back of the shop didn't really cover what I would do once I got there, so I decided to snoop around a bit and hope I'd discover exactly what the Beauty Sisters were plotting.

Then I'd find a way to stop them.

I could hear Trudy still screaming her demands in the shop and, knowing she would continue to scream until she got her own way, I set about a thorough search of the weird cake laboratory.

Starting with the diagrams on the wall.

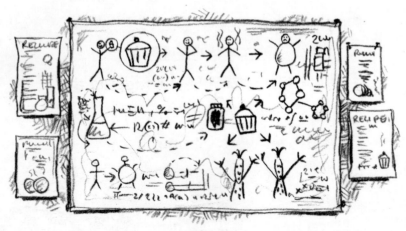

As far as I could work out from the drawings, the twins were filling their cakes with specially modified

fillings that would instantly make people gain weight — which was odd. I'd foiled some strange attempts to take over the world before, but this was definitely one of the strangest.

I also worked out from the diagrams that body heat triggered the swelling of the fillings, which explained why my tampering with the doughnuts had set off the weird expanding jam. But as bodies aren't as hot as radiators, people probably wouldn't explode.

245

They would just get very, very big!

Scattered around the room were large crates filled with cakes and buns, but it was so cold in the lab I decided they were probably harmless so long as I didn't eat them or warm them up. Then I noticed a table in the middle of the room with a large cotton cloth draped over it.

There was no way of knowing what was underneath and it could have been a booby trap, so I pulled out my extendable grabber-hand gadget (which is basically a hand on a stick) and carefully removed the cloth.

Underneath the cloth was the biggest Victoria Sponge I'd ever seen! It was about half my size and stuffed to bursting with jam and cream. Then I peered down at the cake and gasped out loud.

The words 'Happy Birthday Trudy' glared back at me in bright-pink icing!

I could have kicked myself for not making the connection earlier.

Trudy had made a big fuss all week at school about her birthday party – she even held a meeting in the playground where the exclusive party invitations were handed out, along with a typed list of acceptable birthday presents.

Needless to say I didn't get an invitation – and now I was staring at her birthday cake.

Suddenly everything went eerily silent and I realised the sound of Trudy screaming and stamping had stopped. Which could mean only one thing. Either Trudy had just got her own way, or she'd left the shop quietly without getting her own way.

I knew Trudy well enough to know which was most likely and turned round to find two thin figures looming in the doorway!

'Er . . . *Bonjour!*' I said quickly, in my best French accent. '*Croissants?*' I added hopefully, having just exhausted my entire French vocabulary.

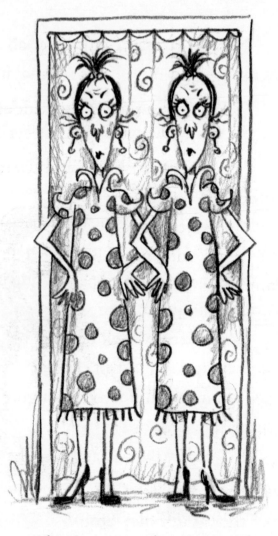

The twins eyed me up and
down and then scuttled forward.

'You're not French,' said the twin on the left.

'You're not chic enough,' added the twin on the right.

I backed away slowly and tried to think fast.

One sure way to buy time with criminal masterminds is to get them ranting about their plans for world domination – most of them can't resist telling you how clever they think they are.

'You won't get away with it!' I said, which is usually a good trigger.

The twins stopped and frowned
at each other; the pair had seen right
through my disguise so
perhaps they were too
smart to fall for the
rant-trigger, and having
backed myself into the
corner of the room I
could only wait and
hold my breath.

'We WILL get away with it!' they yelled in unison. 'Once the world gets a taste of our delicious cakes they'll all puff up like marshmallows, and soon EVERYONE will be a big roly-poly dumpling . . .'

While the Beauty Sisters continued to rant I looked around frantically. The twins were blocking the door so there was no way out –

which meant I had to cause a
diversion to get past them.

My eyes fell on the thermostat
mounted on the wall beside me.

'*Aha!*' I said to myself, because if
I said it out
loud it would
completely
give the game
away. Aiming
carefully I
flicked the
lever on my
extendable
grabber-
hand and

spun the dial from ARCTIC to
TROPICAL, then tucked the gadget
away again in the blink of an eye.

'. . . and when everyone else is waddling around like great big balloons, WE will be the only THIN ones. Then the fashion world will have no choice but to make us supermodels again!' concluded the Beauty Sisters.

'Not bad,' I said, and I said it out loud because I needed to buy more time. 'Except for one tiny flaw,' I added, casually loosening my scarf because the room was already heating up.

'What flaw?' asked the twins suspiciously. 'Our plan is flawless, like us!'

'You didn't count on me stopping you!' I said firmly.

Suddenly a cream horn exploded in the corner of the room,

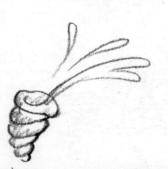

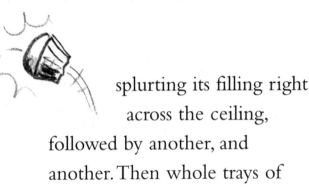

splurting its filling right
across the ceiling,
followed by another, and
another. Then whole trays of
doughnuts and cream cakes started
blowing up all over the place.

BANG!

BANG!

BANG!

SPLAT! SPLAT! SPLAT!

The twins gripped each other and shrieked with each explosion, while I cloaked myself in the cotton cloth and headed for the door, ducking and diving through the minefield of flying fillings.

I was halfway to freedom when the explosions suddenly stopped, and all that remained was the foaming fillings, flowing from the trays.

The angry twins lunged forward but I ducked behind the table in the middle of the room.

Now the only thing that stood between the twins and me was the giant Victoria Sponge. Glancing down I saw that it was already beginning to throb, and the Beauty Sisters had seen it too because they were backing away.

Thinking on my feet I grabbed the giant cake, heaved it above my head and took off after them, which was difficult because it was really heavy.

Then as soon as I was close enough I
lobbed the cake as hard as I could.

I watched in slow motion as the
cake sailed through the air, but the
twins were quick and managed to
duck down just in time. The giant
cake flew over their heads, through
the curtain and out into the shop.

BANG! SPLAT!

The explosion made the curtain flap inwards and through the gap I saw a Trudy-shaped pillar of jam and cream with a sponge on top.

This was quickly followed by an ear-piercing squeal that made the windows rattle.

Trudy did look funny covered in cake, but there was no time to enjoy it. The twins had picked themselves up and now looked even meaner than before. I glanced around frantically and grabbed the nearest things to hand.

Two squeezy bags of bright-pink icing!

With an expert flick of my wrists I cocked the icing bags and aimed them steadily at the twins. The Beauty Sisters immediately put their hands up in surrender – which was just as well because that's when Trudy's parents appeared through the curtain, keen to know why their daughter was buried under a giant cake.

When you're a secret agent you can't hang around and take credit for saving the world, and because all the evidence was there in the cake-lab I quickly armed Mr and Mrs Hart with the icing bags and made my getaway.

I couldn't risk revealing my identity as I passed the creamy, jammy mountain in the middle of the shop. But as two furious eyes peered out at me, I couldn't resist a quick comment either.

'*Bonjour, croissant!*' I said, in my best French accent, and then legged it.